Madelon's Journey

by Ethel Calvert Phillips

Cover illustration by Lydia Colburn
Cover design by Phillip Colhouer
Illustrations by Ilse Martha Bischoff
First published in 1931
Originally titled *Gay Madelon*
This unabridged version has updated grammar and spelling.
© 2019 Jenny Phillips
www.goodandbeautiful.com

Table of Contents

Chapter 1

The Journey Begins

MADELON STOOD IN THE DOORWAY of Madame Le Bel's little white cottage and waited for Papa to take her down to the boat.

Madelon was going on a visit. She was to travel alone on the great river steamboat to Tadoussac to visit Tante Marie and Oncle Paul. At her feet on the doorstep lay her bag, a large yellow bag. Papa had told her many times to keep the bag within reach of her hand while traveling, and with good reason. Did it not hold all Madelon's dresses? Yes, even her new warm frock of red and black homespun, for it might be that Papa would not come for her until the autumn, when already the days would be crisp and cold.

Madelon was a little French-Canadian country girl, or *habitant*, as they are sometimes called. She lived with her father in the tiny village of St. Alphonse on the Saguenay

River, that deep and dark river of the north that moves its way between high, towering cliffs. Madelon had no mother. She and her father made their home with old Captain and Madame Le Bel, who were fond of the little girl and glad to have her there.

This was not strange, for Madelon was as merry and lively a little girl as you might meet. Indeed, her friends and neighbors called her "Bright Madelon," and there is no doubt that she had earned the name.

Her dark eyes were bright and full of fun. Her hands and her tongue were busy all day long. It sometimes seemed as if her feet were never still, those nimble little feet that trotted up and down and in and out on errands or at play. Besides this, Madelon could dance—happy little jigs, whirling measures. Oh, Madelon could keep step to any tune. At the sound of a fiddle, her feet would tap and twitch. But even if

it were only Papa clapping his hands, beating time with his foot, and perhaps singing softly under his breath, Madelon was content. She would dance until Papa tired.

Best of all, she had a warm heart. She loved Papa and Captain and Madame Le Bel dearly. So you see she was a pleasant little companion to have about the house and was loved not only by Papa, but by her friends as well.

But now Papa himself was going on a journey into the far North Woods. He was to guide two gentlemen from the city on a fishing trip. He would not only lead the way through the woods, a way which he knew as well as Madelon knew the roads of St. Alphonse, but he would also show the gentlemen where to fish, he would set up and take down their tent, and he would cook for them. The journey was a long one, and it might be that Papa would be gone for many weeks.

"It would be pleasant for you, Madelon, to visit your Tante Marie in Tadoussac," Papa had said. Tadoussac was a French village far down the river where the Saguenay and the great St. Lawrence Rivers meet. "She has not seen you since you have grown to be such a great, tall girl."

Madelon now measured as high as Papa's elbow. She felt that this was a good height indeed.

So Papa had sent a message to Tante Marie asking whether Madelon might visit her. The message had been carried by Captain Le Bel, who sailed a small boat on his own business up and down the river, and in good time he had brought the answer back.

"Madelon will be welcome at Tadoussac," reported Captain Le Bel. "She is to stay as long as her father wishes and while she is happy and content."

So Madame Le Bel had packed Madelon's bag for her and had risen before sunrise to cook her breakfast and to stand in the doorway to wave her a farewell.

The boat was to sail from St. Alphonse at six o'clock. So it was very early in the morning, not more than half past five, when Madelon and her father, hand in hand, walked down to the dock.

The sun was already shining in the windows of the little gray and white village houses. The sky was softly flushed with pink. A sharp little morning breeze fluttered the ribbon of Madelon's beret and made her scarlet cape fly out behind her like a sail in the wind. Madame Le Bel had set the last stitches in the cape only the day before. She had made it from a piece of cloth that had lain in her trunk for several years.

"Though it is old, the color is as bright and fresh as the day it was made," said Madame Le Bel proudly. She might well be proud, for she herself had spun and woven and dyed the cloth. "I shall not use it for myself now. It is too bright. Madelon shall have a cape. Not a coat; there is no cloth for sleeves. But a cape, yes."

So a cape it was that fitted snugly around the neck and reached almost to the hem of Madelon's frock and with which both Madame Le Bel and the little girl were well pleased.

"I shall miss you, Papa," said Madelon, holding fast to her father's hand as they walked along. "I wish that you were coming with me to Tadoussac."

"I wish so too," was Papa's reply. "But I shall be there before long, and, in the meantime, you will have little cousins to play with you."

"How many?" asked Madelon. "Tell me again."

"Remember that there are as many cousins as you have fingers on one hand," said Papa with a smile. "Hold up your hand and count. First the thumb."

Up went Madelon's thumb as Papa nodded down at her.

"The thumb is Hector," said Papa gravely. "He is the eldest, a happy, laughing little boy with a round, black head. Now the first finger. That is André. He is also a pleasant little boy, but not so merry as Hector, and also with a round, black head."

Here Madelon laughed, for Papa's face wore a comical look.

"The next finger is Germaine," went on Papa. "She is younger than you. I cannot tell you about the color of her hair, for when I last saw her she had none. She was a little baby in her mother's arms."

"But her head is round," spoke up Madelon quickly, "for everyone has a round head."

"Not at all," answered Papa firmly. "Some heads are long and thin like a gourd. But finish with the fingers. Next is little Bernadette. And last of all is baby Victorine. Those two cousins I have never seen."

"Tante Marie and Oncle Paul will love me if I dance and sing for them, will they not?" was Madelon's next question.

She was beginning to feel a little strange now that the moment of parting from Papa drew near.

"They are sure to love you if you are a good girl," said Papa, pressing Madelon's hand close. "Dance and sing by all means, but also be obedient and polite. Run errands for your Tante Marie. She is busy. Save her steps. Perhaps you may rock baby Victorine in the cradle for her."

"Yes, I would like that," said Madelon thoughtfully. "And, too, I might play with Germaine and Bernadette and keep them quiet when they cry."

Madelon felt wise and grown-up as she said this. Was she not a big girl, going on a journey all alone? Surely, no matter what happened, she would not cry like little children, like Bernadette and Germaine.

By this time they had reached the dock, and Papa only nodded absently in reply to Madelon as he led her down the gangway to the boat.

"I must buy your ticket now," said Papa, "and ask someone to see that you leave the boat safely at Tadoussac. Stand close at my side, Madelon, and hold fast to the bag."

Though it was still early in the morning, already many people were astir. On the dock, all was bustle and confusion. Men were wheeling onto the boat trucks loaded with wooden boxes made in the mill at St. Alphonse. Small boys and their dogs stood looking on. They had come down to see the loading of the steamer. They liked the excitement and added to it whenever they could. When the steamer sailed, they meant to jump up and down, fling their caps in the air, and shout.

Madelon knew the boys well.

"There are Pierre and Jean and Victor," she thought.

She smiled and waved her hand, and the boys grinned shyly back at her and dug their toes into the cracks of the wharf.

On the boat people were moving about. Most of the passengers were up early this morning. They wished to sit on the decks and gaze at the cliffs on either side of the dark river,

cliffs that sometimes showed the green of windblown pine trees and sometimes bare, gray rock.

By and by, the steamer would reach the two highest cliffs, Cape Trinity and Cape Eternity. Then the boat's whistle would be blown, and the echoes from among the hills would answer, once, twice, three times. Of all this Madelon had often heard. Today she was to see it for herself.

Now Papa turned and, taking the yellow bag from Madelon, led her up the wide stairway to the deck. There he settled her in a chair with the precious bag under her feet.

The boat's whistle shrieked. It was the first warning that the steamer was ready to sail.

Papa bent and kissed Madelon, once on either cheek.

"Be a good girl, Madelon," he said, looking into her eyes. "I will come for you soon."

Then, smiling so cheerfully that Madelon smiled bravely back at him, Papa hurried away.

The whistle shrieked again.

There stood Papa on the dock below. He was smiling and waving his hat to Madelon.

There were shouts and cries, and slowly, softly, the great white boat moved away from the shore and out into the bay.

The journey to Tadoussac had begun.

Chapter 2
The Journey Ends

ON THE WHARF Papa still smiled and waved, and
Madelon, now at the rail, threw kisses back to him with both
her hands. Pierre and Jean and Victor shouted and leaped
up and down and flung their caps in the air. The dogs barked
wildly, their noses pointed to the sky.

Smaller and smaller grew Papa and the boys. Wider and
wider stretched the water between Madelon and the shore.
How different St. Alphonse looked as they moved farther out
into wide Ha Ha Bay! Instead of the familiar cottages and
mills and stores were tiny gray and white houses clustered
at the water's edge or nestled on the hillside. The lonely little
village in this far northern land seemed chill and desolate, in
spite of the morning sunshine, to the other travelers on the
boat. But not to Madelon, for to her it was home.

The boat swung round and moved slowly out of the bay. It
headed down the river toward Tadoussac.

Papa and the boys and the wharf were now out of sight.

Madelon sat very straight and still in her chair. She pressed her hands tightly together. Of course she was a big girl, a very big girl, traveling alone. Of course she did not mean to cry. But how strangely she felt! So suddenly it had come upon her too! Her throat hurt her. It was shut so tight she could scarcely breathe. She wanted more than anything in the world to run back to St. Alphonse, to hold fast to Papa's big, strong hand. She wanted to see kind Madame Le Bel and the captain and even Pierre and Victor and Jean.

A tear rolled suddenly down Madelon's cheek. She wiped it carefully away. She rubbed her cheek with her handkerchief. No, no, she would not cry. A pair of long legs flashed past her. They belonged to a little girl. Madelon leaned forward and watched her run out of sight around the corner of the deck. The little girl wore a blue and white dress. Her hair was red, oh, very red, and it blew out in the wind.

Presently the little girl rushed past again. This time she did not turn the corner, but, with her eyes fixed on Madelon, climbed boldly up the ladderlike stairway that led to an upper deck. Madelon watched the nimble legs until they disappeared. She wished the little girl would come back. She looked both lively and happy.

It was not long before the nimble legs of the little girl appeared on the stairway again. The little girl was coming down, and she led a lady by the hand.

Along the deck they came, past Madelon, and here the little girl stood still.

She smiled in a friendly way, and then she said something that Madelon could not understand. She spoke in English, of that Madelon was sure, for there were English people at St. Alphonse.

Papa and the boys and the wharf were now out of sight.

The little girl spoke again and pulled her mother's hand. She seemed to be asking a question, and Madelon shook her head.

"I do not speak English," she said politely. "I speak only French, you see."

At this, the little girl's mother smiled pleasantly and answered her in French.

"With my daughter it is just the other way," she said. "She cannot speak French. She speaks only English. But I can tell you what she says. She wishes to know your name."

"My name? My name is Madelon, Madelon Duval," said the little *habitant* girl. "Will you not tell me hers?"

The lady sat down in a chair nearby, and at this Madelon's face brightened into a smile. How pleasant to have someone talk to her! No longer was she lonely. No longer did her throat feel sore. It made her happy now, not homesick, to think of visiting Tante Marie.

"My little girl's name is Virginia," began the lady, "but we call her Ginger, for short, because of her red hair. She wishes to know where you are going and why you sit here alone."

So Madelon gladly told about Papa and the fishing trip and Oncle Paul and Tante Marie. She told of Madame Le Bel and the new scarlet cape and even of Hector and André and Germaine, whom she had never seen. All this, whenever Madelon paused for breath, Ginger's mother told to the impatient little girl, who jumped up and down in her eagerness to hear.

"We are Americans," Ginger's mother in her turn told Madelon. "We have come all the way from the city of New York to see your Saguenay River. But now Ginger wishes you to walk with her about the boat. Will you not go with her up and down the deck?"

Madelon shook her head.

"My bag—I cannot leave it," she said.

"I will keep it for you," said Ginger's mother. "I will keep it by my side."

Madelon eyed her closely.

"It holds all my dresses," she said doubtfully, "even my new warm dress of red and black."

"I will keep my hand upon it," promised Ginger's mother with a smile. "I will sit here in your chair and watch it as if it were my own."

So Madelon, glad to stretch her stiff little legs, went off with Ginger. It was pleasant, too, for a time, to be free from the care of the big yellow bag.

It was surprising, though the little girls could not talk to one another, how simple it was to make themselves understood. They pointed and nodded and laughed, and when it grew really too funny, they ran to Ginger's mother for help.

They were glad, too, to stand beside her at the rail when the boat moved slowly past the two great mountains, Cape Trinity and Cape Eternity. Huge cliffs of stone, gray rock, and twisted weather-beaten pine, they soared straight above the dark water, higher and higher into the sky. Madelon and Ginger held tightly to one another as they looked up and up and thought that they would never see the top.

It was very quiet as the boat moved in under the cliff of Cape Eternity, and the little girls were quiet too. The great sight filled them with awe, as it did the other travelers. They, too, looked up and up and were quiet. If anyone spoke, it was almost in a whisper, it seemed.

Then, suddenly, the boat whistle blew.

Back from the hills rolled the echoes, hollow and fearful and shrill. Three times the captain blew his whistle. Three times the echoes answered with a shriek and cry that rolled from hill to faraway hill.

At last the sounds died away, and they steamed out from under the mountain and went on their way down the river again.

They were not far now from Tadoussac, where Madelon would leave the boat and her new-found friends.

When Ginger heard this, she chattered eagerly to her mother and then rushed off down the stairs. Presently she came back with a little basket in her hand, a sweetgrass basket of bright red and blue.

"Ginger wishes to give you this basket," said her mother, as Ginger, unable to wait, pressed it into Madelon's hands. "She wishes you to have it so that you will not forget her, your little friend from faraway New York."

Madelon's face was bright with pleasure. She turned the basket round and round in her hands. How sweet it smelled! How pretty too!

Suddenly Madelon leaned forward and kissed Ginger on the cheek. Then, down on the deck, she knelt beside the big yellow bag. Carefully she opened it and, feeling in the corner under the new red and black homespun dress, drew out a small silver medal on a long black cord.

"It is St. Christopher," explained Madelon. "He takes care of those who go on a journey."

She slipped the cord over Ginger's head and stood back to admire the gleam of bright silver on the blue and white frock.

"Now," said Madelon with a nod, clasping Ginger's hands, "we shall never forget one another. Is it not true?"

She closed the bag tightly again. As the boat prepared to swing around into the harbor at Tadoussac, a steward, who had been asked by Papa to watch over Madelon, came to carry her bag and see that she was met safely as she left the boat.

Ginger and her mother went down with her, too, and stood at her side as the boat neared the shore.

The wharf was crowded with people. Everyone in Tadoussac, it seemed, was there to see the boat come in.

Eagerly Madelon looked from face to face. There were many men and boys and dogs. There were ladies and children, all in bright summer dresses too. How should she know Oncle Paul and Tante Marie? Suppose no one met her and she was left sitting alone on the wharf with her big yellow bag?

The boat was made fast and the gangplank thrown down.

Madelon had said goodbye to Ginger and her mother.

The steward held her hand ready to lead her off the boat when suddenly Madelon gave a cry.

"I see them! I see them all!"

Yes, she did. There they stood in a row—Oncle Paul, thin and dark, Tante Marie, pretty and plump, Hector and André

There they stood in a row.

with round, dark heads, Germaine, and Bernadette, and yes, in Tante Marie's arms, was baby Victorine. There was no mistaking them.

And they saw Madelon.

Tante Marie hastily handed the baby to Oncle Paul. She pressed forward to the gangway, and as Madelon, her cape and ribbons flying, ran off the boat, she was caught in Tante Marie's outstretched arms.

Her journey to Tadoussac was at an end.

Chapter 3

In Tadoussac

ON THE WHARF stood a long line of open carriages, some of them painted a bright orange or green, others a more sober black or brown. To one of these carriages, so lovely in its coat of green that no one would notice where the harness was well mended with bits of rope, Tante Marie led Madelon.

"This is the carriage of your Oncle Paul," she said, "and every day he comes to meet the boat and perhaps take the tourists for a drive. There are many others who do the same, as you may see. But this morning there will be no tourists, for the boat is sailing now. So your Oncle Paul means to drive us home instead."

Into the back seat climbed Tante Marie, and beside her were lifted Madelon, Germaine, and Bernadette. There was plenty of room, for the little girls sat close as they were bidden, and of course sleeping Victorine, in Tante Marie's arms, took up no space at all.

On the front seat were Oncle Paul, very straight and dark, and the boys Hector and André, whose heads were quite as round and black as Papa had said. Their eyes were very black, too, and bright, as Madelon soon found, for they both turned around and stared over the back of the seat at her as if they had never seen a little girl before.

In spite of this, Madelon did not feel strange, for on one side small Bernadette held fast to her hand, and on the other smiling Tante Marie asked many kind questions about Papa and Captain and Madame Le Bel.

Madelon herself was smiling as she looked about. It was all so pleasant, so sparkling and bright.

Oncle Paul's big brown horse, Roland, took them briskly along the sandy road. Overhead the sky was a deep, bright blue with not a cloud in sight. The sun sparkled on the water that seemed bluer than the sky. Above the water, the seagulls flapped and circled and floated by. The sunshine turned the seagulls into silver. It made the curving yellow beach shine like gold. The beach was dotted with little children digging and running to and fro and with ladies sitting in the shade of brilliant parasols, orange and green and scarlet, every hue.

Madelon longed to join the children on the beach. Never before had she seen anything so colorful.

But now they were riding past a red and white building, a long, low building with many windows gleaming in the sun. And about the building grew great beds of flowers, yellow and orange and glowing scarlet too.

Madelon leaned forward with a little cry of pleasure. Such flowers did not grow at home in St. Alphonse, of that she was sure.

"This is the great hotel, where people come from far and wide to stay," said Tante Marie a trifle proudly. "And nowhere else do the flowers grow so beautiful and so large."

"We look at them, but we never pick them," said a small voice—"never!"

The small voice belonged to Germaine, who, having spoken, turned her shoulder upon Madelon and looked down into the dust of the road. Germaine was very shy. But she already had smiled once upon her new cousin and now, having spoken, no doubt would soon be more friendly.

"I will not touch the flowers," promised Madelon earnestly. "But I would like to walk past them and look and look."

"So you shall," said Tante Marie kindly. "And you shall also go to the Indian Chapel which we are passing now. There is something beautiful in there that I know you would like to see."

Madelon gazed at the little Indian Chapel with its snow-white walls and red roof and the old bell hanging in the tiny turret topped by a slender cross.

"Something beautiful in there? What is it, Tante Marie?" Madelon was ready to ask this question when suddenly Hector spoke.

"Do you sing?" demanded Hector. "Tell me, do you sing?"

"Yes, I sing," answered Madelon. "Papa has taught me. I dance too. Why? Do you wish to have me sing and dance?"

Hector nodded. "It is well that you sing," he told her, "for now you can go down every day when the boat comes in and sing by the roadside. Many children go, you will see."

"Why do they sing when the boat comes in?" asked Madelon. "Why?"

"They sing for the pennies that the tourists give them," was Hector's reply. "The tourists come walking up from the boat to visit the Indian Chapel or to buy homespun that we have made during the winter. And there, by the roadside, they find the children singing and, both coming and going, they give pennies to those who please them by their song."

Madelon nodded when Hector spoke of the tourists. She had seen these travelers at St. Alphonse when they left the boat and walked about the town.

"What can you sing?" asked André with the air of a little schoolmaster. "Tell us the names of the songs that you know."

"I can sing the song 'In the Pale Moonlight' that tells of Columbine," answered Madelon. "That is my favorite song. And I know 'On the Bridge at Avignon,' and 'Sleep, Bébé, Sleep,' and many others as well. Do you go down to sing, Hector and André? Will you and Germaine come and sing with me too?"

Hector spoke first. "I sing, and I also dance," he said, laughing at the thought. "I do not sit with the girls at the roadside. I stand below on the sand. I sing the 'Marseillaise' and caper about. The tourists laugh and throw pennies down to me, and I sometimes think that the worse I sing and dance, the more pennies they throw."

Madelon laughed with him. He was a merry little boy, as Papa had said.

"And Germaine?" questioned Madelon, looking around at her cousins. "Tell me, do you sing?"

Germaine's only answer was to put her finger in her mouth and look down at the toes of her shabby shoes. But Hector was quite ready to answer for her.

"Germaine is too shy to sing," he volunteered. "But now that you have come, she will go with you and hold the purse, I have no doubt."

"What does André do?" inquired Madelon.

How pleasant it all seemed, singing and dancing and gathering pennies in a purse!

André was able to speak for himself.

"I carry bags and bundles for the tourists," he said. "I meet the boat every day at the dock. I am strong, and I carry the bundles well. I do not sing or dance," said André gravely, shaking his head. "I am not amusing, and the tourists wish to be amused."

André would have been surprised if he had known how many extra pennies had been slipped into his hand because these same tourists had been amused by his funny, businesslike airs.

"We all serve the tourists, one way or another," announced Hector. "You should see the homespun that my mother makes to sell them, blankets and scarves and rugs."

"It is the most beautiful homespun in all Tadoussac," spoke out the small voice again.

And this time Germaine looked around and smiled directly at her new cousin Madelon.

All this while, Oncle Paul had spoken but little. With his pipe between his teeth, he had driven steadily up the sandy, hilly road, with only an occasional flick of the whip or shake of the reins or cry of "Ha! *Houp-là! Vite!*" to guide his tall, brown horse.

Now he pulled in the reins and brought his carriage to a standstill before a small white house with a narrow veranda running across the front.

"Home!" said Oncle Paul briefly and helped his family to dismount.

Within, Madelon found the cottage to be very like that of Madame Le Bel. There were the four square rooms with a steep stairway leading to a loft overhead. There was the great loom on which was woven the homespun, blankets and rugs and scarfs. In the corner stood the brown spinning wheel, polished with long years of use. The sink, the pump, the table, the bench—Madelon was familiar with them all, as she was with the lovely flowered wallpaper ornamented with a bright-colored calendar and even brighter pictures of the saints. And, too, Tante Marie was quite as proud of the coarse, white lace window curtains that covered the shining panes of glass as was Madame Le Bel in her home.

But there was something to be seen in Tante Marie's kitchen of which Madame Le Bel could not boast: a cradle, a stout wooden cradle, that swung to and fro with a comfortable creak.

"Perhaps I may be allowed to rock Victorine as Papa said," thought Madelon, moving the cradle to and fro with a gentle hand. "That I would enjoy, but most of all, I wish to go and sing at the boat."

Aloud she asked, "Do I go today to sing by the roadside?"

Tante Marie smiled at the question and shook her head.

"Not today, but tomorrow," said Tante Marie.

Chapter 4

By the Roadside

EARLY THE NEXT AFTERNOON, everyone made ready to go down to meet the boat, everyone, that is, except Tante Marie and Victorine and little Bernadette.

First Oncle Paul, sitting very straight, his small black mustache turned up sharply at either end, drove off in fine style, the green carriage newly washed and spotless. Roland, in spite of his years, showed a spirit equal to the day and pranced out of sight down the road with a great flourish of heels and swishing of tail.

André departed next, feeling the muscles of his arms as he went.

"I grow stronger every day," he called back to Madelon. "The heaviest burdens are nothing to me."

Madelon and Germaine, hand in hand, followed Hector down the road. Madelon wore her scarlet cape, for the day

was cool, and under it her play dress of black, prized by
Madame Le Bel because it did not show the dirt, covered by a
bright-colored apron.

"I will find you good places," promised Hector, "and
for your part, Madelon, you must sing loudly, and you,
Germaine, must hold out your hand."

"Germaine is carrying my new basket for the pennies,"
said Madelon, "my basket that was given to me yesterday on
the boat by the little American girl."

Hector eyed the basket, clutched in Germaine's small
hand, and raised his eyebrows.

"It looks large to me," decided Hector. "It might frighten
the tourists. I think I should hold out my hand."

Germaine, behind Hector's back, shook her head. She
meant to hold out the red and blue basket. The very sight of it
would make the tourists wish to drop pennies, many pennies,
into it, she felt sure.

Down the sandy road Hector led them, past the Indian
Chapel, already with its door ajar, past the great hotel
overlooking the curving yellow beach. Then came a few
houses, some large, some small.

Across the veranda of the very smallest house, a tiny
yellow cottage with blue window shades and white curtains
of lace, were hung a number of bright homespun rugs.

"In that house," volunteered Hector, pointing it out with
a nod, "lives our friend Madame Pinaud. The tourists stop
at her house to buy. She sells my mother's homespun for her
because we live too far from the boat."

"Are those Tante Marie's rugs hanging on the veranda?"
asked Madelon.

"Yes, and Madame Pinaud's too," was the reply. "We will
stop there on our way home. There is a little lame boy staying
with Madame Pinaud this summer while his sister works

at the big hotel. You will like him. We all do. His name is
Jou-Jou. Now here are the children by the roadside, as I told
you. Do you see?"

Along the road that wound its way down to the wharf
sat children in little groups of two or three or alone. Hector
knew them all and pointed them out by name.

"These three, they do not sing," said Hector with a wave
of his hand toward three tiny girls who huddled in a row like
birds on a bough. "They sit and look frightened and each
one holds out a large, open purse. They are Cécile, Blanche,
Gabrielle. For my part, I would not give my penny without a
song."

Madelon smiled at the three solemn little ones who
managed to give back a timid smile or so.

"Over there sits Marcel," continued Hector, nodding
toward a plump little boy, round and rosy as an apple. On his

small lap he held an accordion so large that it almost hid him from view.

"Ho, Marcel!" shouted Hector. "Give us a tune."

Marcel obligingly set to work. With a great jerking of arms and a swaying to and fro, he pulled the accordion out and pushed it in, making dismal, rumbling sounds. It was not necessary for Hector to murmur behind his hand, "You see? He cannot play."

They passed a group of children, whom Hector described as "laughing as much as they sing," and then neared a thin-faced little girl who sat alone. Madelon's eyes grew round with pity when Hector whispered that she was alone because she might not share her pennies with a friend.

"Her father gets upset with her if she does not bring home enough to please him," confided Hector, "but we all share with Marguerite when she needs help and have saved her from a tongue-lashing many times."

Now Hector halted and looked about him.

"This is the place for you," he said. "I can see you from the sand, and you are not too near the other children. Sing your best, Madelon. Sing your loudest and best. But look! Here comes the boat! I must run!"

Off sped Hector, and Madelon saw him jump from the road down onto the sandy beach.

Everyone was looking across the little bay at the great white river steamboat that made its way slowly, like a huge swan, toward the wharf. In the afternoon, the boat came from the big cities of Montreal and Québec far up the St. Lawrence River. The next morning, the same boat stopped on its homeward way from St. Alphonse, Madelon's little town. In either case, the boat was crowded with tourists, and today, in the height of summer, they seemed to fill every chair and line the railings on every deck.

Again the wharf was crowded with men, boys, ladies, and children. "City people from the hotel," thought Madelon, and rightly. It was not hard to pick out Oncle Paul, standing in the long row of carriages beside the greenest carriage of all. As for André, there he stood at the edge of the wharf, ready to carry the bundles of the very first passenger who stepped ashore.

Nearer and nearer drew the great white boat. The whistle shrieked. Slowly, slowly, the boat drew into the wharf. There was the rattle of chains, the slap of the heavy ropes thrown round the posts on the dock. Down went the gangplank with a thud.

Here come the tourists! Here they come!

Madelon and Germaine held one another's hands. How exciting it all was! What would happen next?

First of all came the carriages. One by one, the horses galloped up the road at a smart pace, slowing down as they turned the corner by the Indian Chapel, then off again at a run. There was no time to be wasted if the countryside were to be seen. The boat would stay at Tadoussac only an hour or less.

"Our carriage," breathed Germaine as Oncle Paul came driving by.

There were several people in the carriage, laughing and talking and looking about. Oncle Paul did not turn his head. You might have thought he did not see Madelon and Germaine sitting by the roadside. But of course he did. He saw them quite well.

Next came the tourists who chose to walk, plowing their way through the deep sand of the hilly, uneven road. There were young men and women and older people, too, laughing and talking happily and looking about as they stepped along. They all seemed interested and pleased at what they saw.

Indeed, everyone wore a happy, holiday air. It was a happy scene—the pleasure-seeking tourists; the dancing, singing children; the bright sunshine; the blue water touched with sparkles of gold.

Below the road on the sand stood Hector, capering about and waving his arms. He sang the "Marseillaise" as the tourists went walking by.

"Ye sons of France, awake to glory!" sang Hector, and many people stopped to listen.

He did very well until he came to the high notes. These he could not sing at all, so he laughed instead. This did just as well, for the tourists laughed too. They liked the merry, black-haired little French boy, whose black eyes danced with fun. They flung pennies down to him, and Hector caught

them neatly. Not one did he lose in the sand. And every time he caught a penny, he made a bow.

On came the tourists in little groups of twos and threes and fours.

Then Madelon began to sing. She sang the old nursery song of Columbine who runs in the moonlight to the door of her friend Pierrot. Ever since she was a baby, Papa had sung this song to her, and Madelon knew it well.

> "In the pale moonlight
> To thy door I run.
> Lend a pen, I pray thee,
> Till my task is done.
> Candlelight I have none,
> Burns my fire no more,
> For the love of Heaven,
> Open now thy door."

Madelon liked the song, and the tourists liked it too. They stopped to listen. They smiled at the little *habitant* girl sitting by the roadside with her bright black eyes, her dark curls, and her cheeks that were almost as red as her bright scarlet cape. They laughed and dropped pennies into the red and blue basket that Germaine held tightly in her lap. They did not understand. English words they were, such as Ginger knew. Madelon's eyes were bright. Her cheeks grew very red.

Now, who should come marching along the road beside two stout ladies, one of whom walked with a cane, but André. His arms were empty—not a bundle. But it was not hard to guess that soon he would be coming back laden with the purchases that the ladies were to make. He pretended not to know Madelon and Germaine. He walked with head erect and chest thrown out to show how strong he was.

No sooner had the last tourist gone up the road and vanished into one of the houses that sold homespun—perhaps Madame Pinaud's—or into the Indian Chapel, or the quaint and beautiful hotel, than the first tourists began to come back down the hill again.

All along the road could be heard the children singing and the dismal wheezes made by the accordion of plump Marcel. Madelon sang and smiled; Hector capered and laughed. The pennies dropped into the red and blue basket. How pleasant it was!

The boat whistle sounded a warning, and down the road came the tourists in a hurry, as fast as they could walk.

André appeared with his two stout ladies, though really you could see very little of André under his load of blankets and rugs. When he neared Madelon, he walked with a quick, light step to prove that the heaviest burdens were nothing to him.

Now the carriages came rolling down the hill. Oncle Paul again passed them with an air as if they were strangers. This made Madelon laugh. It was such fun.

The boat whistle blew again, once, twice. The passengers were all on board. The gangplank was drawn up. Slowly the boat steamed out into the river, round the corner, and out of sight.

Now everyone moved homeward. The wharf was soon deserted, not a person to be seen. The ladies strolled back to the hotel, and the children ran down to the beach. The men and boys went about their affairs. The carriages rolled away. The boat had come and gone. The excitement of the day was over.

Madelon rose to her feet. She waved happily to Hector running toward them over the sand.

"I think," said Madelon, smiling down at little Germaine, who was still clutching the basket, "I think that to sing by the roadside is the most pleasant thing in the world."

Chapter 5

At Madame Pinaud's

STRAIGHT UP THE ROAD toward Madame Pinaud's went the children.

"This was a good day," said Hector gleefully, peering into Madelon's basket. "Have you many pennies? Oh, you are rich! I can count six, eight, ten—there are at least twelve pennies, perhaps more."

Madelon smiled with pleasure as the basket, shaken by Germaine, gave out a merry, jingling sound.

"I liked the singing best, but I am glad of the pennies too," said Madelon, "and I should like to give some of them to Marguerite, if I may!"

"Marguerite?" Hector shook his head. "There she goes up the hill, laughing. It has been a good day for us all, I tell you. My own pocket is full, for one."

It had been a good day at Madame Pinaud's, too, it proved. She met them in the doorway with a smile.

"Tell your good mother," she said at once to Hector, with a hand on his arm, "that I have sold her blue rug with the orange border. She will be glad of the news, for it was the largest and best that she made. It was bought by a stout lady, led here by André, who is a good and sensible boy for his years. She bought also my rug of green and two blankets. It is well."

Hector looked as pleased as Madame Pinaud. He knew how hard his mother and the other women of the village had worked all winter, making homespun for the summer tourists to buy. Now it was good news, indeed, to learn that the tourists had done as it earnestly had been hoped they would.

"So this is Madelon." Madame Pinaud looked down upon her kindly. "Come in, come in, and see our little Jou-Jou and his big sister, Louise."

The little lame boy sat on his sister's lap, his head thrown back against her shoulder and a half-finished string of buttons dropping from his hand to the floor. To string buttons was Jou-Jou's pastime. When he had finished two strings or three, he took off the buttons and began over again.

He was a fair little boy, with hair that curled softly around a face that was far too thin and white and a pair of brown eyes that seemed to ask the other children, "Why is it I may not run and play like you?" One leg was weak and almost helpless. A little crutch stood in a corner of the room, but Jou-Jou liked best to be carried in the strong arms of his sister, and failing them, to sit still in his chair.

Louise Martel and her little brother, Julien, whose tender pet name was Jou-Jou, a toy, lived alone in Québec, where, as a seamstress, she earned a slender living for them both. But this summer she had come to work in the big hotel at Tadoussac, and Jou-Jou, for a very small sum, was looked

after by Madame Pinaud. Every moment free from her tasks at the hotel was spent by Louise with the little boy, for they loved one another dearly. In his four short years, he had known no other mother and Louise no other happiness than in caring for him. In her struggle to earn a living, Louise had known loneliness and hunger and cold. But her spirit was brave, and her love was strong, and the faith that a happier day would come never failed her.

Madelon looked from the boy's delicate little face to that of his sister who held him so tenderly in her arms.

"Oh, she is pretty, so pretty!" thought Madelon.

She liked the fair hair and the gentle brown eyes, the sweet smile, and the low voice which said, "See, Jou-Jou, here is a new little girl come to make friends with you."

Madelon smiled brightly. She could think of no better way of making friends. Her warm heart was filled with pity for this poor little boy. She longed to do something to help him, to make his leg well and strong. Oh, if Papa were only here! Papa could do so many wonderful things. But Papa was far away in the Great North Woods, and Madelon could do nothing but show her friendliness with a smile.

But her look was so merry and her smile so bright that Jou-Jou's answering smile almost turned into a tiny laugh.

"Have you a name?" asked Jou-Jou in a fine little voice. "No one has told me your name."

"She is my cousin," interrupted Hector, who never could be silent long. "Her name is Madelon."

"Let me look at this little girl." Madame Pinaud sat down in her low rocking chair and drew Madelon to her side.

"My dear," said Madame Pinaud, looking closely at Madelon with her sharp black eyes, "my dear, I knew your mother well when she lived here, a young girl, with your Tante Marie."

"I do not remember Maman," said Madelon, shaking her head. "I was a tiny baby, of no age at all, when she went away to heaven, so Papa says."

"You look like your mother," said Madame Pinaud with a nod, "the same dark eyes, the same red cheeks, the same smile. Your mother sang. Her voice was sweet. And she danced, light as a feather. I can see her now."

"Madelon can dance. At least she says she can," said Hector with a teasing laugh. "And she can sing. That I have heard for myself."

"For shame, Hector," said Madame Pinaud, smiling as she shook a finger at the naughty boy. "Will you not dance for us now, Madelon? It would give pleasure to us all."

"Jou-Jou will like to see dancing," spoke out Germaine from her quiet corner, "and I shall like it too."

"Yes, dance, dance!" piped up Jou-Jou in an eager voice. "Louise, will you not like to see the little girl dance?"

Madelon was delighted at the idea of dancing. There was nothing in the world that she liked better to do.

"Who will clap and sing for me? As Papa does?" she asked, smiling around the room. "Can you do it, Hector, do you think?"

Hector was quite willing to try.

"Is it like this?" he said. "This is a tune that the fiddlers played at the big wedding here in the spring, when Marie Corday was married to Pierre De Bois. It goes so."

And Hector, his head on one side, began to whistle a lively tune. Madelon listened, her eyes bright, her hand keeping time.

Hector finished with an extra trill, and Madelon, pleased and excited, exclaimed, "Yes, yes, I can dance to that air, I am sure! But you must clap and tap your foot as well. I will show you how."

Hector learned quickly, and in a few moments Madelon, her bright apron making a bit of bright color in the room, took her place on the floor.

Hector was seated on Madame Pinaud's low bench, hands lifted, foot raised, lips pursed.

"Ready!" cried Hector. "Begin!"

And to the notes of the bright little tune, the steady clapping and the tapping, Madelon began to dance.

To and fro, back and forth tripped Madelon, her twinkling feet never missing a step. She whirled and she twirled, light as a butterfly, swift and graceful as a bird. Her curls bobbing, her cheeks very red, Madelon danced on and on, now fast, now slow, now fast again.

As for Hector, manfully he entered upon his part of the performance. He whistled his tune, he clapped his hands, he tapped his foot with enough energy for half a dozen boys instead of one. Out of breath? No. Tired? Never. Hector was happy as arms and foot and head kept time to the tune.

Eyes bright, cheeks glowing, Madelon danced with so much spirit, she tripped so lightly on her toes, that she seemed more like a graceful cherub than like a little girl. Her feet kept time to the music that beat steadily on and on until presently everyone in the room fell under the spell. Louise and Madame Pinaud began softly to tap the floor. In her quiet corner, Germaine clapped her hands to help the music too. And from his sister's lap, Jou-Jou wagged his curly head and clapped his tiny hands in time with the rest.

They were all clapping and nodding and tapping when Hector's breath gave out, and with a last whirl the dance came to an end.

"Bravo! Bravo!" cried Louise. "Clap your hands, Jou-Jou! Clap for Madelon!"

Jou-Jou clapped his loudest, quiet Germaine in her excitement hopped up and down, while the musician so far forgot himself as to stamp both feet and shout.

But it was Madame Pinaud who surprised them all and quite took Madelon's breath away.

She rose from her chair and walked out to the middle of the floor where Madelon stood.

"My dear," said Madame Pinaud solemnly, "you are a dancer, a real dancer. Someday you will dance upon a stage. A real audience will clap for you."

Then, quite as solemnly, Madame Pinaud walked back to her chair and sat down.

Chapter 6

The Indian Chapel

THAT WAS THE END, for the afternoon, of the dancing at
Madame Pinaud's.

Jou-Jou, hoping to keep these pleasant guests, begged for a
song from Louise.

"About the clear fountain and the nightingale," coaxed
Jou-Jou, patting his sister's cheek, "or the one about 'rolling
my ball' that I like so well."

But Louise shook her head.

"Another day, little Jou-Jou," she answered, "and very soon.
But now I must go. There is much mending for me to do at
the hotel."

"We must go too," said Hector. "My mother will be
wondering where we are."

"Do not forget to tell her about the rug," called Madame
Pinaud as they ran down the path, Louise in her blue dress
hurrying on ahead.

Madelon's thoughts were of Jou-Jou as the children walked along. Her warm and loving heart held the wish that she might do something to help this little boy. Suppose it were she herself who could not run about and jump and play! Suppose, oh, suppose, that she were lame and could not dance! Good little Jou-Jou! He had not said one fretful word nor uttered one complaint. When they left, he had waved goodbye to them all from his little chair in the doorway, and then patiently had gone back to his stringing of buttons. What could Madelon do for him? What could she do?

Beyond the hotel, amid coarse grass and behind a white picket fence, stood the little red and white Indian Chapel.

Madelon looked with interest at this quaint old building. Not yet had she been inside, but she remembered what Tante Marie had said, "something beautiful in there that Madelon would like to see."

"Hector, do the Indians come here to church now?" she asked. "I have not seen any Indians here in Tadoussac."

Madelon had seen Indians in St. Alphonse, however, for they, like her father, sometimes acted as guides in the Great North Woods.

"No, not now," answered Hector. "The chapel was built for them by the good missionaries from France many years ago. That was when there were no white men, only Indians about."

"Does no one come to church here now?" asked Madelon. "Could I not come some day and see inside?"

"It is open for church only once a year, on St. Anne's Day," replied Hector, "and that is past. But it is open for the tourists, and the door is ajar now. Sister Joséphine must still be inside. She comes every day with Sister Rose-Claire when the tourists are here. Perhaps she will let you come inside. Wait here!"

Hector climbed the steps and disappeared into the chapel. Presently he came out on the doorstep and beckoned the little girls in.

"Yes, you may come in," he said softly, "but only for a moment, Sister Joséphine says."

The little girls tiptoed through the doorway, and Madelon found herself standing before a great drab curtain that shut off all view of the church.

Timidly she walked around the curtain into the little chapel with its carved altar and narrow, old-fashioned pews and tiny pictures hanging along the walls. Sister Joséphine, quick of step and brisk of manner, nodded in reply to Madelon's curtsy and took her by the hand.

"It is growing late," said Sister Joséphine, "and you children should be at home. But there is something over here that this little girl will like to see."

Just what Tante Marie had said, "something beautiful that Madelon would like to see."

Sister Joséphine led Madelon to the side of the chapel. On the wall, as high as the little girl's head, was fastened a dark wooden box with sides of glass.

Eagerly, Madelon looked through the glass.

In the box lay a "Little Jesus," a beautiful wax baby dressed in a fine robe of silver and lace, more rich and delicate than anything Madelon had ever seen.

"Our Little Lord," said Sister Joséphine in a quiet voice.

Madelon did not speak. She was gazing in at the "Little Jesus" who lay so sweetly there as if asleep. She had forgotten Hector and Germaine. She had forgotten Sister Joséphine, too, until she heard her speak.

"This 'Little Flower' was sent here to the Indians many years ago," said Sister Joséphine's voice. "He was given to them by a great king, King Louis the Fourteenth, who lived

ILSE BISCHOFF

far over the sea in France. And this beautiful robe, too, was
made by the hands of a queen."

The beautiful robe! Yes, it was beautiful, all silver and
ribbon and lace, made with tiny stitches, each one set with
love and care, no doubt. Madelon and Hector and Germaine
stood gazing in at the "Little Flower." Though Hector and
Germaine had seen this "Little Jesus" many times, they
stood quietly looking at the pretty sight. As for Madelon, she
felt as if she could look and look and never tire. There was
something about the sweet mouth, the tiny hands, that made
her think of Jou-Jou. It was this baby, so weak and yet so
powerful, Madelon had been taught, who could heal Jou-Jou
and make him strong and well.

43

But Sister Joséphine was ready now to lock the door of the Indian Chapel. It was time to go.

As Madelon turned, she caught sight of a box for offerings of money fastened above the "Little Flower." She knew well what it was for. Did she not drop a penny every Sunday into just such a box at the church in St. Alphonse?

Quick as a flash Madelon emptied her red and blue basket of its precious hoard of pennies.

One by one she dropped them into the box.

"I give them to the 'Little Jesus,'" said Madelon trustingly, "because I hope He will make Jou-Jou's leg strong and well."

"A beautiful hope," was Sister Joséphine's answer, "and, if it is for the best, no doubt He will."

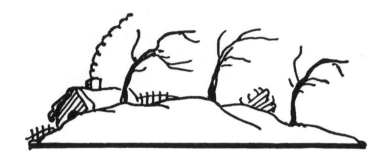

Chapter 7

Summer and Autumn

SUMMER IN TADOUSSAC! And Madelon had quickly learned how many pleasures there were to be enjoyed at this season of the year.

"When I go home to St. Alphonse, I shall have much to tell Madame Le Bel," said Madelon one day when they were spending Louise's free hour down by the water's edge. "I shall tell her first of singing by the roadside, for, after dancing, that I like to do best of all."

Madelon still went almost every day to sing for the tourists. The red and blue basket showed signs of wear, so many pennies had been dropped into it by tourists who liked to hear the fresh little voice and see Madelon's bright and smiling face.

"Will you tell Madame Le Bel of the day we all went blueberrying?" asked Germaine.

"And of the seven pails of berries we picked, filled to the brim?" added Hector.

The day they had gone blueberrying was one long to be remembered. For one thing, Louise had been given a holiday by the housekeeper at the hotel. For another, the day had been sparkling and bright, a day such as only Tadoussac can give, when everyone feels lively and happy and strong.

From Madame Pinaud and Tante Marie down to little Jou-Jou and Bernadette, they had all picked and eaten to their hearts' content. Even Victorine, with the juice of a few berries spilled into her tiny mouth, had laughed and waved her arms and entered into the spirit of this gala day.

And afterward what tarts had been baked, sweet and juicy! What tempting jars of jam now stood in a row! Not to mention the bottles of blueberry juice that would be drunk next winter at *fêtes* and on Saints' Days and at the good New Year.

Often they clambered over the rocks to sit by the water, and there they caught glimpses of the white whales that sported about quite close to the shore. Once or twice, they

had seen the flat black head of a seal, who found the chilly waters of the St. Lawrence and the Saguenay quite to his northern taste. There were boats, moving slowly up and down, on pleasure or on business bent. And the mewing seagulls, wheeling and flapping and sailing by.

Sometimes they journeyed to the nearby woods where it was pleasant to lie on the thick pine needles and look up through the tall tree trunks at the faraway blue sky. There the children gathered pine cones for Jou-Jou, who lay happily at his sister's side, sifting the fragrant pine needles through his fragile hands.

And always, wherever they went, Louise sang. She knew many of the old songs of the French-Canadian folk, and those that Jou-Jou liked best she sang over and over again. "By the Clear Fountain," where the nightingale sang and the roses bloomed, was Jou-Jou's favorite. But the sad fate of the white duck shot by the king's son in "Rolling My Ball" also touched his heart. Madelon and Hector listened and sang with her and soon knew some of the songs almost as well as she.

But pleasant times must come to an end. Summer waned and autumn drew near. The big hotel was emptying fast. The children must go back to school. People were hurrying to the cities and their homes.

At last, the day came when Louise and Jou-Jou were to go home to Québec. Her work at the hotel was at an end. Another summer and they might come back to Tadoussac. But now Louise must search for sewing she could do at home, for she could neither leave Jou-Jou nor take him with her to her work.

She stood on the wharf with Jou-Jou in her arms, the children clustered about her, loath to say goodbye.

"Oh, Louise," mourned Madelon, Jou-Jou's hand pressed against her cheek, "when shall I see you again? If you come to Tadoussac next summer, I shall not be here."

"Perhaps you will come to Québec," suggested Louise with a smile. "Listen while I tell you where I live. Sous-le-Fort Street. The Street Under-the-Fort. Can you remember that?"

Madelon nodded. "Yes, indeed. The Street Under-the-Fort. But how should I know your house? Would you be looking for me from the door?"

Louise shook her head, but she did not smile at Madelon's simple question.

"There will be no need of that," she said. "This is how you will find me. Walk along the street and look in the windows. When you see a blue chair with a blue cushion, say to yourself, 'That is Jou-Jou's chair.' Look on the windowsill. There will be a yellow pitcher standing there. And in the pitcher will be—"

Louise paused.

"Harlequin!" shouted Jou-Jou in a voice that would not have startled a mouse. "My dolly! Harlequin!"

"It is his little harlequin doll," explained Louise. "He lives in the yellow pitcher. It is his home."

"Harlequin will be glad to see me because I bring him a present," announced Jou-Jou, shaking a large bag of pine cones that the children had gathered for him. "He will be sure to like them, for we have no pine cones in Québec."

"Do not forget," called Louise as she and Jou-Jou went on board the boat. "Come to see me, all of you, if you are in Québec."

And as the boat moved out into the bay, Louise at the rail, with fluttering handkerchief, called once more, "Sous-le-Fort Street! Do not forget!"

Before Summer had quite turned her back on Tadoussac, Autumn was knocking at the door.

"Papa will be here soon," said Madelon when the leaves on the trees turned yellow and red, when the ground in the morning was silvered with frost, and there was a thin glaze of ice on Roland's drinking trough. "Now, in the autumn, is the time that Papa will come."

But instead of Papa, who, one day, should come walking into Tante Marie's house but Captain Le Bel. He carried two great bundles, one in either hand.

Madelon ran straight to him.

"My papa," she asked, "is he here? No? Then is he coming soon?"

Captain Le Bel lowered himself into the chair that Tante Marie dusted for him with her apron. He drew Madelon between his knees.

"It is this way," began Captain Le Bel. "Your Papa has gone fur trapping into the woods."

Madelon knew very well what this meant. Last winter, Papa and another man had gone trapping far, far into the north. They had lived in a tent, with a small iron stove to keep them warm, and about them had been nothing but the woods and snow and bitter cold. Papa had brought home many skins of otter and beaver, mink and muskrat. Later had been made for Madelon a cap and coat of beaver skins, warm, very warm.

"This is your father's message," went on Captain Le Bel. "You are to stay here with your Tante Marie, if she will keep you, until after the New Year. Your father will then go to Québec to meet the man who has ordered these skins of him. And you, my little Madelon, are also to go to the great city of Québec and join your father there. Now, what have you to say to all this?"

"I shall see Louise again," was Madelon's first thought.

But, after that, there were many questions that she must ask.

"Will my father meet me in Québec? Where shall I sleep? If the boat does not run, how shall I reach the big city of Québec?"

Captain Le Bel put his hands over his ears. "Enough! Enough!" cried the captain. "One question at a time, if you please. You are to stay in Québec with your father's old friends Monsieur and Madame Coté. They have known your father since he was a boy, and he calls them Père Coté and Mère Clotilde. What next?"

"Will my father be in Québec to meet me when I come?"

"Perhaps yes, perhaps no," was the captain's answer. "Your father will have a long journey on foot through the woods before he can reach a horse and sleigh. He cannot say just what day and hour he will reach Québec. But he will meet you there, sooner or later. Do not fear. What next?"

"How shall I reach Québec when the boat no longer runs?"

Madelon knew that soon now the river would be covered with ice.

"You will go by sleigh and perhaps by train. Is it not true, Madame?" And Captain Le Bel looked at Tante Marie, who nodded in reply. "But all these matters, Madelon, you may safely leave to your good aunt. These two bundles hold your winter clothing. They are sent by Madame Le Bel. Now I have business to talk over with your aunt about which you need not bother your head."

Madelon was not listening. She was smiling to herself.

"I shall see Papa and Louise in the great city of Québec. And that is well," thought Madelon.

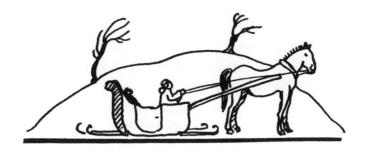

Chapter 8
The Sleigh Ride

IT WAS WINTER NOW, midwinter, well past the New Year, and Tadoussac was held fast in the iron grip of ice and snow.

It had been beautiful in summer, with the green of the hills, the blue of sky and water, and the gold of the sands. The autumn had brought splendor: gorgeous red and yellow, orange and russet brown. But now, set amid hills of purest white, ringed round by fields of snow, the village showed a frosty loveliness, almost like a storybook at times. The little houses took on a new grace under their caps of snow. The great trees bent beneath their white burden, the icy river sparkled in the sun, and the frozen roads, marked out with branches of evergreen, made iron music beneath the horses' hoofs.

Madelon, in the autumn, had watched Oncle Paul make ready for winter. He had packed earth and boughs on the ground around the house and barn to keep out the cold. The old sleigh had been mended and skillfully touched up here and there with paint. There was a huge woodpile behind the house that reached the eaves.

Indoors, Tante Marie had been busy too. Already had she begun her winter weaving. The hum of the spinning wheel had sent the children to sleep night after night, and Tante Marie spent long hours at the loom. Down from the loft had come the bed of Hector and André. No one would sleep far from the stove now that winter was at hand. Rags were stuffed into cracks, papers nailed over thin places in the wall. And none too soon.

For one morning, Tadoussac opened its eyes upon a white world, a hushed and quiet world. The snow was falling in thick white flakes. The ground, the trees, were covered with snow. The windowsills were heaped high. Winter was here.

Now the wind, the strong north wind, the bitter north wind, began to blow. It piled the snow in drifts, man high— house high at times. It blew the snow into the house, sifting it through the cracks of windows and under the door. It tossed the smoke from the chimneys like torn feathers hither and yon.

It was very cold, a bitter, biting cold. Snow everywhere! Winter in Canada!

It was past the New Year, and Madelon stood before Tante Marie, listening intently to every word that she had to say.

"You are to start for Québec tomorrow morning early," said Tante Marie. "You are to travel in a sleigh with the son of Madame Pinaud. He has little ones of his own at home. He will take good care of you."

Madelon waited, her eyes fixed upon Tante Marie.

"It will take three days or more to reach Québec," continued her aunt. "If it snows, I do not know how long you will be on the way. It is a long journey for a little girl. I wish that your father had waited until the spring. But—he is your father, and he knows."

Here Tante Marie shrugged her shoulders. Madelon's father had willed it. There was no more to be said.

"Am I to ride on the train?" asked Madelon.

Tante Marie shook her head.

"The train costs much money," she said. "Madame Pinaud's son will go straight to Québec. It is better that you should travel with him all the way."

"And at night," asked Madelon, "do we sleep in the sleigh?"

"Tst-tst-tst!" was Tante Marie's answer. "Would you freeze to death? You will sleep in the houses of friends of Monsieur Pinaud along the way. And now to bed, while I pack your bag. This has come suddenly. You were not thought to go until next week."

Snuggled cozily in her bed between Germaine and Bernadette, Madelon listened to the wind howling around the house, to the boards that snapped with the cold, and to the hum of the great stove, stuffed with logs, that steadily sang and sometimes roared its song of comfort and of warmth.

"I shall see Papa and Louise," thought Madelon drowsily. "I shall—"

And almost the next moment, it seemed, there was a touch on her arm, and there, beside the bed, stood Tante Marie, a lamp in her hand.

"It is morning," Tante Marie was saying. "Hurry, Madelon, the sleigh will soon be at the door."

But Madelon was ready and waiting when, with a jingle of bells, Monsieur Pinaud brought his sleigh to a standstill before the house. Indeed, she had kissed Tante Marie and Oncle Paul and all the children twice round and had said goodbye many, many times.

It was a low sleigh, called a cariole, set on heavy wooden runners and with a high back to keep off the wind. It was well lined with bear skins, and Monsieur Pinaud was so covered with furs that one could scarcely see the tip of his nose.

"Is the little girl well wrapped?" he shouted as the door opened and Madelon ran down the snowy path.

"Indeed, yes," called Tante Marie, in the doorway, from out the folds of her shawl. "If she wore more, she could not walk."

This was almost true. Madelon, under her fur coat and cap, wore two dresses, three pairs of stockings, and leggings long and warm. On her hands were rabbit skin mittens. On her feet, moccasins lined with fur.

Oncle Paul put her bag, her large yellow bag, into the sleigh and tucked the robes snugly around her. Madelon sank back into what seemed like a warm nest of fur.

A snap of the whip, a jingle of bells, and the sleigh moved off. Madelon heard Tante Marie shut the door. She knew that the children were peering out at her through the frosty windowpane.

Goodbye, Tadoussac! Goodbye, Tante Marie and Oncle Paul and all the children! Goodbye!

Madelon drew a long breath and looked up at the sky. The stars were shining with a faraway cold gleam. All about them, in the dimness of the early winter morning, stretched a snow-white world. It seemed a different world from that of every day. Even familiar Indian Chapel looked strange in this chilly light of early dawn.

Madelon stole a glance at Monsieur Pinaud. He turned and smiled down at her.

"Are you comfortable," he asked, "and warm?"

He was a stout man in a black fur cap with eartabs and with a mustache that grew in many directions, not sharply pointed at the ends, like Oncle Paul's.

"It will be a clear day," said Monsieur Pinaud pleasantly, pointing with his whip toward the east, where now showed the red streaks of a winter sunrise. "We must hope for good weather, and no snow, so that our journey will not be too long."

The horse trotted steadily on, bearing them swiftly over the snow-packed road. The sleigh bells jingled merrily. The wind blew in their faces, but Madelon was shielded by the big fur robe.

Every now and then Monsieur Pinaud looked down and asked, "Are you comfortable and warm?"

They passed a tree with a large hole in the trunk, and Monsieur Pinaud again pointed with his whip.

"An old friend of mine lives in there," said Monsieur Pinaud with a solemn face.

"A friend? In a tree?" And Madelon peered up over the edge of the robe.

"A friend," repeated Monsieur Pinaud stoutly, "a little black bear who loves me so well that he sent me a present at the New Year. It was a present of honey that the bees had left in his tree."

Madelon and Monsieur Pinaud laughed heartily at this joke. A pleasant friend, the little black bear, they both agreed.

Not long after, Madelon pulled her arm from under the robe and waved a mittened hand toward the roadside.

"In that tree yonder," said Madelon "lives my friend. He is a squirrel, and for the New Year he sent me a bag of nuts!"

All the rest of the journey, they pointed out the homes of their friends in the snow caves or hollow trees along the way. And there was no telling at what moment they might not spy the friend himself, rabbit or squirrel, bear or wolf, peeping from his own front door.

At noon they stopped at a lonely house for a meal. Madelon was glad of the hot soup that warmed her through and through. In the afternoon, the warmth and motion of the sleigh and the sound of the bells made her drowsy. She took little naps, and because of them, the time passed quickly. She was surprised when Monsieur Pinaud drove up to a farmhouse and said that here they were to spend the night.

The wife of the farmer was kind to Madelon. After supper, she undressed the little girl and put her to bed with two of her own children, older girls who tried on Madelon's rabbit skin mittens and admired her red and black dress.

The next morning, they made an early start. The day was clear, and Monsieur Pinaud was high in spirits. He pointed out a cave where the rabbits had had a party the night before, he said, and he talked for a long time of his two little boys and baby girl. Madelon, in return, had many stories to tell of St. Alphonse and Tadoussac. And in the afternoon, to pass the time, she sang, but very softly, so as not to disturb her companion, who was smoking his pipe and seemed to be deep in thought. But he must have been listening, for presently he put his pipe in his pocket.

"I know that song," said Monsieur Pinaud, joining in the chorus.

After that, they sang together the songs that Louise had taught Madelon, and Monsieur Pinaud caroled alone a bright tune that the woodcutters sing in camp.

It was all very pleasant. The stout little horse, who seemed to be tireless, sped over the roads that were hard and free from drifts. The sky was clear. There was not a sign of a coming storm.

"If the sun shines tomorrow, we shall be in Québec by nightfall." Monsieur Pinaud said this over and over again as he scanned the horizon for snow clouds. "Never before have I made such good time on a trip."

The next morning, the stars glittered in a cloudless sky as the travelers, well rested after a good night's sleep, drove off in the dawn.

All day, Madelon talked and sang and took little naps that refreshed her and left her feeling bright and happy. The morning was clear, but in the afternoon a haze crept over the sky and, looking at it sharply, Monsieur Pinaud shook his head.

"That may mean snow," he said gravely. "In that case, we might be delayed one, two, perhaps three days. It will be better to press on to Québec tonight, even though we are late in reaching there."

And Monsieur Pinaud drove straight to a little roadside inn and, jumping from the sleigh, lifted Madelon out.

"We will eat and stretch our legs," he said with a smile, "and feed our good horse and give him rest. Then we will start on the last leg of our journey, and before the clock strikes ten tonight, you will be in Québec, your ride at an end."

In the winter dusk, Madelon and Monsieur Pinaud set forth together for the last time. Madelon was tired now, in spite of the rest and the hot meal at the inn. She slipped down in her seat with her head against Monsieur Pinaud's arm.

"Sleep, then," said her friend's voice, very far away. "Sleep and rest."

Madelon sat up with a start and peered over the edge of the robe. Where was she? Awake or dreaming?

She was still in the sleigh. There was the jingle of the bells and steady motion as they slid swiftly over the snow.

Eagerly Madelon looked about. Was this Québec? Was this the great city? Oh, how many houses set close together, row on row! How bright the tall street lamps, making some places as light as day! How many people and horses and sleighs!

Tadoussac was never crowded like this, even when the boat came in.

Monsieur Pinaud pointed with his whip.

"Look, Madelon! Look!" he said.

Before her, high in the air as if on a mountaintop, rose a great building, a beautiful castle, blazing with lights from end to end. There was a huge tower, gleaming in the darkness, that rose higher and higher into the sky, far above the spires, the many turrets, and the pointed roofs below. There were row upon row of windows in this castle, and in every window sparkled a brilliant light. And before the castle glowed great lamps, each one as large as the moon.

"It is the Château," explained Monsieur Pinaud, "the great Château. Someday you will be taken there to see it, no doubt."

Monsieur Pinaud shook his whip, and the sturdy little horse sprang forward.

"Do not sleep, Madelon. We are almost there."

But, in spite of this warning, in spite of the splendid Château, Madelon's eyes would not stay open. Her head nodded. She slipped down in her seat. In another moment, she would have been fast asleep if the sleigh, with a last merry jingle, had not come to a standstill before a house in a narrow street.

Madelon felt herself lifted from the sleigh. A pair of strong arms carried her indoors and up the stairs. Someone undressed her and put her in bed.

"Is my papa here?" murmured Madelon, trying to open her heavy eyes.

"Not yet. He is coming," said a voice.

Then Madelon knew no more, for after her long, long sleigh ride she had fallen sound asleep.

Chapter 9

New Friends

THE NEXT MORNING, Madelon woke to the sound of a fiddle playing a happy, rollicking little tune. But before she could slip out of bed and find the music, it stopped, a door opened and shut, and all was still.

Madelon climbed down from her high feather bed and crept to the window. She parted the stiff white lace curtains and looked out.

Across the way were narrow, uneven houses, set side by side in a row, not an inch of space between. Lace curtains were in the windows, colored oilcloth on the doorsteps down to the walk. The narrow street was deep with snow and the roofs and dormer windows were snowy too.

Madelon pattered out of the room and down a long, narrow hall. All Père Coté's rooms were on one floor, it seemed.

At the end of the hall, Madelon stepped into a kitchen where a shining black stove gave out a pleasant warmth, where a canary bird, hanging in the window in his golden cage, swung merrily on his perch.

A tall woman with rosy cheeks and black hair parted down over her ears stood ironing in the sun. This was Mère Clotilde, and when she caught sight of Madelon standing in the doorway, she set down her iron with a thump and took the little girl in her arms.

"The little Madelon!" said Mère Clotilde warmly, patting and rocking her to and fro. "Come on such a long journey to meet her papa in Québec! Your father will be here soon, and until then you will be happy with Père Coté and me."

"The fiddle," said Madelon. "I heard a fiddle play."

"Oh, ho! You like the fiddle?" and Mère Clotilde caught Madelon close. "It was Père Coté who plays a little tune each morning before going to his work. If you like the fiddle, you and Père Coté will be good friends. But now for your breakfast."

It was a strange way to eat breakfast, for Madelon, well wrapped in a shawl, sat up to the kitchen table, and Mère Clotilde talked as Madelon ate, and every now and then she gave her a little hug.

"It is long since I held a little girl in my arms," said Mère Clotilde, smoothing Madelon's head, "and yet at one time I had nine little boys and girls of my own. That is why we are still called Père Coté and Mère Clotilde, their father and I."

"Where are they now?" asked Madelon. "Do they live with you here?"

"No, no, not one. They are scattered far and wide. They have grown into men and women," explained Mère Clotilde with a little sigh. "They have homes of their own, and all of them far away."

"And Père Coté? Will he come home tonight?"

"Indeed, yes," was the answer. "Père Coté is a porter who carries heavy bags and trunks for the guests at the great Château. The Château is a hotel. The Château Frontenac it is called."

"I saw it!" cried Madelon, dropping her spoon. "I saw it last night from the sleigh. There were many lights, and it was beautiful. Will I go there one day, do you think?"

"Without a doubt," answered Mère Clotilde, smiling at Madelon's excitement. "Père Coté will take you within the Château someday when he has time, and this very afternoon you shall go with me and we will walk around it, if you like."

Mère Clotilde, besides keeping the house, did fine washing and ironing as well. And that afternoon, with Madelon holding fast to one hand, she set out to carry a great bundle of snowy laundry to one of her ladies who lived not far from the Château.

Now you must know that the old French city of Québec is built on a cliff. The part of the city that stands on top of the cliff is called the Upper Town and that lying below the cliff, the Lower Town. That is where Père Coté and Mère Clotilde had their home.

Up the steep flight of stairs, called Breakneck Steps, that leads from the Lower to the Upper Town, climbed Mère Clotilde and Madelon. And there at the top, facing the great St. Lawrence River which sparkled like a jewel in the sun, stood the beautiful Château.

"It is built like an old French castle," said Mère Clotilde with pride. "People come from all over the world to visit here. See the high tower and the turrets and the pointed roofs. Look through the arches at the great courtyard where the sleighs stand before the door."

Madelon held fast to Mère Clotilde. She had never before seen so many sleighs, so many people, so much passing and re-passing in the streets.

There were many sights around the Château for Madelon to see. Here in Québec, it was plain, people enjoyed the ice and the snow and were glad to be out in the fine, bracing air that made them tingle and glow with the cold.

There were skating rinks where merrymakers skated and glided and danced to the sound of lively music. There was a steep toboggan slide down which came the long sleds, laden with young folk laughing and shouting with fun. Bright sleighs, bearing happy loads, skimmed up and down the steep streets to the silver music of bells.

And behind all the gaiety and color and laughter, high on the hill, dark against the afternoon sky, stood the Citadel, the great grim fort, with its flag flying in the winter wind.

Mère Clotilde explained this in answer to Madelon's questioning look, and at the word "fort," Madelon caught Mère Clotilde's hand with both her own.

"It is there that my friend lives!" cried Madelon. "The Street Under-the-Fort! I could not remember the name of the street this morning, you know, when I told you of Louise and little Jou-Jou, who cannot walk. The Street Under-the-Fort! Is it here, Mère Clotilde, that she lives?"

"The Street Under-the-Fort," repeated Mère Clotilde. "Is it so? Then your friends are but round the corner from where you are living now. Down to the corner, over the way, round another corner, and you are there. It is truly the Street Under-the-Fort below the cliff. Tomorrow morning, Madelon, you and I will go together and find your friend Louise and her poor little brother who is lame."

It was this good news, "Louise is nearby," that Madelon told to Père Coté when he came home that night.

"It is well," replied Père Coté with interest. "And, once found, your friends must come to see us here. The young lady sings, you say? Perhaps she will sing to my fiddle."

And sitting on the old-fashioned settle in the kitchen, Père Coté tucked his brown fiddle under his chin and prepared to play.

Madelon crept upon the settle beside him. On her knees she whispered in his ear.

"I, too, sing," whispered Madelon shyly, "and I also dance."

"It is too good to be true!" exclaimed Père Coté happily, laying his fiddle across his knees and putting an arm about Madelon. "Not since my little Mimi grew up and married have I had anyone in my house who could sing and dance. What can you sing? What will you dance? What shall I play for you?"

Mère Clotilde sat by and laughed at them both. Pleased and excited, they did not know where to begin. Père Coté's blue eyes twinkled; Madelon's black eyes danced. Père Coté ran his fingers through his gray hair till it stood out like a halo. Madelon's cheeks burned, and her feet tapped the floor.

Oh, what merry, rippling little tunes Père Coté could play! Full of trills and runs that taught Madelon new steps without anyone saying a word! Sometimes the airs were lively so that Madelon whirled like a leaf dancing in the autumn wind. Sometimes they held a plaintive note like those of the lonely birds who fly seeking a haven on the cliffs of Madelon's own dark river of the north. Such music! Such dancing! Mère Clotilde dropped the stocking she was knitting and clapped and clapped again.

Then Madelon sang. And of all the songs that Papa had taught her, and the songs that Louise had sung, Père Coté could play them, every one. How different the fiddle made them sound, so rich and full and deep! Columbine's song, "In the Pale Moonlight," that Madelon had sung by the roadside, seemed far more sweet when the fiddle crooned softly too.

When the songs were ended, curled on the settle at Père Coté's side, Madelon sat and listened to stories of the great Château, of the beautiful rooms, of the wide halls, of the great ballroom with its shining floor and gleaming lights and chairs of gold.

"Shall I go there one day, do you think?" asked Madelon with longing. "Shall I see the beautiful rooms and the golden chairs and the fine people walking to and fro?"

"Someday I will take you there," promised Père Coté. "You will see all the beauties of which I have told you and many more. Now, 'to bed' your Mère Clotilde is saying. And, once safely there, I will play you a song for goodnight. When you hear it, you will think of little children snug in their beds and the angels watching over them all through the night."

"May the angels guard you too," said Madelon. "Goodnight, Père Coté, goodnight."

Chapter 10

The Street Under-the-Fort

IT WAS JUST AS MÈRE CLOTILDE HAD SAID, "down to the corner, over the way, round another corner," and you found yourself in the Street Under-the-Fort.

This Madelon knew, for early the next morning she and Mère Clotilde set out, and, by following these directions, there they were in the street they sought without any trouble at all.

It was a narrow little street, lined with narrow, crooked little houses. It was all old, you could see at a glance. But, one good thing, the windows were low, and Madelon could peer into most of them without even standing on tiptoe. Which was well, for Madelon was looking for Jou-Jou's blue cushion and blue chair. She was looking, too, on every deep windowsill, that were wide, very wide—for oh! how thick

were the walls!—looking for the yellow pitcher with Master
Harlequin standing inside.

Madelon was peering into every window on one side of
the way as they walked, and Mère Clotilde had offered to
look over the street on the other.

"Madelon," said Mère Clotilde when they had passed not
half a dozen houses, "see, over there! Is not that a blue chair
standing in the window?"

Madelon looked. It was! It was! There, too, on the
windowsill stood the yellow pitcher, and in it, peeping
jauntily over the edge, was a harlequin, shabby and very

small, to be sure, but a harlequin, nevertheless, in scarlet and black and white. Unmistakable!

As they looked, a pair of arms lifted someone into the blue-cushioned chair. And when Madelon caught sight of the little white face, the softly curling yellow hair, the thin little neck, she dropped Mère Clotilde's hand and ran straight across the street.

"It is Jou-Jou! It is Jou-Jou!" she cried. "Louise! Louise! Let me in! It is I, Madelon! Let me in!"

She danced up and down before the window waving both hands.

Jou-Jou saw her. For a moment, he did not know who it was, but only for a moment. Then his face lighted, he dropped his string of buttons on the windowsill, he clapped his hands, and called out, "Madelon! Madelon!"

Louise's face showed for a moment over Jou-Jou's head. Then the front door was flung open, and Madelon threw both arms about her friend's neck.

In the narrow front room, which, with one other, was all Louise and Jou-Jou had for a home, Mère Clotilde sat and watched the three friends who had not seen one another for so long a time.

Madelon had so much to tell. She talked of Tadoussac and the friends living there, of her long ride to Québec, of why she came, and where she was staying, and what she had seen.

As Madelon chattered on, Mère Clotilde glanced around the bare, shabby room. It was poor, very poor. Louise's dress was threadbare. She herself looked thin and pale.

"Perhaps the little boy is always frail, but I believe they do not eat enough good, nourishing food, those two," thought Mère Clotilde wisely. And who should know better than she, who had brought up nine children, all of them living and well? "They have no money."

Madelon looked. It was! It was!

And, leaning forward, Mère Clotilde smiled in a friendly way and gently asked a question or two.

"You are a seamstress, our little Madelon says?" queried Mère Clotilde politely. "And perhaps you have not too much work on hand at present?"

"No, not too much work," was Louise's honest answer. "It is difficult to find sewing to do at home, and I cannot leave Jou-Jou nor take him with me, as you see."

"That is true," agreed Mère Clotilde kindly. "But I asked with reason. I myself do fine laundry work, and often among my ladies will be one who wishes sewing done. If you have the time, I will speak to them, if you wish."

"I shall be glad of work," was Louise's answer. "It has been a hard winter for me."

"Indeed, yes," agreed Mère Clotilde again. "I shall do my best for you. Come, Madelon."

Madelon and Jou-Jou were busy just then with Master Harlequin.

"He was pleased with the pine cones," Jou-Jou was saying, "as I thought. See, we play with them every day."

There were the pine cones on the windowsill arranged in row after row.

"They are soldiers," said Madelon quickly. "Is it not true? And Harlequin is the captain, perhaps."

"We take turns at being captain, he and I," answered Jou-Jou gravely. "Now I must tell you about the New Year. But put Harlequin back in his pitcher first, so that he may not hear."

Madelon stood Harlequin in his strange little roofless house, over the edge of which he smiled so cheerfully out.

"It was this way," said Jou-Jou in a low voice. "I wished for a toy at the New Year. All the children have them here, you know. There was a beautiful dog, with long white fur and a red tongue, in the shop down the street. I wished for that dog. But Louise said it would make Harlequin feel bad. He might think that I loved the dog more than I loved him."

"That is very true," agreed Madelon.

Jou-Jou nodded, with a fond glance Harlequin's way.

"So I had bonbons instead, at the New Year," he finished with a smile. "I am glad now that I did not hurt Harlequin's feelings. But I did wish for the little dog."

"Come, Madelon," interrupted Mère Clotilde. "We must go. But ask the little Jou-Jou if he and his sister will have supper with us tomorrow night. Père Coté will play his fiddle, and perhaps we can have singing and dancing and a little laughter too."

It was very exciting the next evening when Louise and Jou-Jou came to supper at Mère Clotilde's. Père Coté had hurried home and changed his black porter's blouse for a splendid jacket of velveteen. Mère Clotilde had cooked a fine supper, chicken and pancakes, and a deep apple tart. Madelon could scarcely sit still in her seat at the table, so great was her excitement and joy. Louise's cheeks grew pink as she laughed and talked. And Jou-Jou smiled happily round the table as he busily plied his fork and spoon.

But the pleasantest time came after supper, when they settled down in the cozy kitchen while the winter wind howled without and the stars gleamed coldly down upon the snowy street. The fire in the stove sent out a cheerful glow. The canary in the window chirped sleepily from his golden cage.

Mère Clotilde spread a bright red and white cloth over the table and sat down beside the lamp with Jou-Jou in her arms. The little boy, warm and comfortable and well fed, leaned back against her broad shoulder and drowsily eyed them all.

Madelon and Louise sat hand in hand. What happiness to be among friends!

Père Coté tucked the brown fiddle under his chin.

"First, a few little tunes," said Père Coté.

And he played for them lovely airs, soft and sweet, and stirring tunes, such as soldiers know and sing. He played music that made them think of the spinning wheels to be found all about the countryside, and music that told of happy children rising higher and higher in a swing, and then music that was deep and solemn, such as you might hear in church.

Every kind of a tune, to suit every taste, did Père Coté know and play.

Last of all, he slipped into a lively, lilting jig.

"Is it for me?" asked Madelon eagerly. "Am I to dance for you all?"

At a nod, she stepped into the middle of the floor, and a second later was lost in the pleasures of her dance.

A bright-eyed little figure she was in her red and black homespun dress, her bobbing curls, and her round-toed little shoes that twinkled merrily to and fro. Old steps and new steps, Madelon did them all. The fiddle sang now high, now low, while Madelon danced for her friends to her heart's content.

Père Coté drew his bow sharply across the strings in a final chord. Madelon made a wide curtsy. The dance was done.

"Now," said Père Coté, looking at pretty Louise from under his bushy gray eyebrows, "a song? A little song? This one you know, I am sure."

Yes, Louise knew "By the Clear Fountain" and sweetly sang it through.

It was Jou-Jou's favorite song. He sat up straight and opened his eyes wide so that he might not lose a word. He never tired of hearing of the clear fountain, of the nightingale singing in the oak tree, and of the rosebush and the beautiful lost love.

There were many other songs of Canada and Old France that Père Coté played and that Louise sang for them. Her voice was sweet and true. She sang with sparkle and dash. She was not pale and tired now. Her eyes were bright, her cheeks pink. She looked bright and happy, without a care.

At last, Père Coté put down his bow. He nodded and smiled as if pleased.

"This winter, at the Château, they are giving concerts," said Père Coté quietly. "For the guests, you understand, in the evening. The guests dance until they are tired. They then sit at small tables and refresh themselves, and while they are resting, they listen to a song."

Mère Clotilde stopped rocking Jou-Jou to and fro. Louise fixed her eyes upon Père Coté, who was looking directly at her as he spoke.

"It is the plan at the Château this year," went on Père Coté, "to have an *habitant* from the neighborhood come and sing his songs. Last week, there were two woodsmen who sang the songs of the logging camp. They wore their logging dress, boots, heavy shirts, and all. Their voices were good, and they gave pleasure."

Père Coté paused, but no one spoke.

"They have someone who will sing at the concert this week," continued Père Coté, "but next week there is no one. That, I happen to know. And it may be, only *may* be, that they will engage you to sing if I spoke a word. But only if you wish it," he added hastily. "Only if you wish it, you understand."

"I do wish it," answered Louise. "I wish it with all my heart."

Père Coté wagged his head and ran his fingers through his hair.

"Good! Good!" he said heartily. "They pay, you know. They pay well. I cannot tell you the sum, but it is good. Have you a costume?"

"Yes, a French dress, a peasant dress, I wore at a *fête* once, but it fits me still. Would it do?"

"Admirably! Admirably!" answered Père Coté. "But, understand, I make no promises. I have yet to ask and explain and talk at length and see this man and that. You must not be disappointed if nothing comes of it. Promise me you will not be disappointed. Promise!"

Louise smiled, and Madelon laughed outright. What a bright, jolly fellow was Père Coté!

"I promise," said Louise, pressing her hands together in her lap. "But, oh! I hope this good chance will come to me."

"I hope so too," was Père Coté's reply.

And Mère Clotilde, from under the lamp, nodded earnestly too.

"It will come, this good chance," said Madelon confidently, with an arm about Louise's neck. "There is no one who sings so sweetly as Louise. No, not in all Québec. The good chance will surely come. I think it," said Madelon.

Chapter 11

The Good Chance

MADELON RAN THROUGH THE FROSTY STREETS, her cheeks and her fingers tingling with cold. Straight to the Street Under-the-Fort she hurried, and with only a hasty wave of the hand to Jou-Jou, peering with faithful Harlequin from the window, she knocked upon Louise's door.

"Louise!" she cried before she had stepped over the sill. "Louise, guess why I am here! Guess what news I bring! Guess!"

"Is it good news?" questioned Louise.

But she need not have asked, for Madelon was smiling, and her eyes were big with pleasure and bright. Surely no messenger of bad tidings ever came with so blithe and merry an air.

"I will tell you," spoke out Jou-Jou from above his string of buttons, in his blue-cushioned chair. "It is that Louise is to sing at the Château."

Since the evening spent with Père Coté and Mère Clotilde, Louise had talked often to Jou-Jou of her great hope that she might sing at the Château. Small wonder then at Jou-Jou's guess. The thought had filled both their minds from morning until night.

"Oh, Madelon, tell me, is it true?"

Louise looked as if she could not wait for an answer. But at Madelon's quick nod and smile, she covered her face with her hands.

"Louise, are you crying?" Jou-Jou, with a troubled face, stretched out his little arms. "I thought that you wished to sing. Do not cry."

Louise turned and caught Jou-Jou up in her arms. She was not crying. She was smiling, but Madelon saw that her eyes were wet.

"Indeed, I do wish to sing, my little Jou-Jou, my own little jewel," said Louise, holding him close. "I am not crying. I am laughing because I am happy. Is it true, Madelon? Is it true that I am to sing?"

"Yes, it is true," Madelon told her, putting her arms about Louise and looking up into her face. "You are to sing one week from today in the evening. At the great Château, Louise. Think of that! I have not been inside it yet, but I am to go before long. It is promised me. There are golden chairs, Louise, and sparkling lights, and everyone in the Château is beautiful and kind. Père Coté tells me stories of it almost every night."

"What did he say about my singing, Madelon?" asked Louise. "Tell me every word. What message did he send?"

"He came into my room this morning when I was in bed," reported Madelon. "He was playing the fiddle. He was laughing, and it sounded as if the fiddle were laughing too. You know what I mean, the tune was so lively and bright."

"Yes, yes, I know," nodded Louise. "Go on."

"He stood at the foot of my bed," went on Madelon, "and while he was playing he talked to me. He said, 'Get up, lazy one, and run to the house of your friend Louise. Tell her that one week from now she is to sing at the Château. Tell her that the great ones of the world and those that are rich, very rich, will listen to her. And that if she gives pleasure this time, it may be she will be asked to sing again.'"

"Did he say that?" asked Louise, her face radiant. "Oh, Madelon, my good chance has come!"

"Indeed, yes," agreed Madelon, "and you will be the prettiest one there. That I know. Père Coté will see you tonight, he said. Now I must go, for I have not eaten yet. I ran straight here as soon as I was dressed."

"Oh, Madelon, what a good friend you are!" cried Louise.

"Because I love you," answered Madelon.

For the next few days, there was much running back and forth between Mère Clotilde and the Street Under-the-Fort.

Père Coté and Louise practiced the songs together night after night, for he was to play his fiddle when she sang. They had long talks, too, in which Mère Clotilde joined, as to what might happen if Louise gave pleasure that night.

"She will surely be asked to sing again," said Mère Clotilde.

"Perhaps not once again this season, but twice," added Père Coté. "I shall be proud of her, never fear. And I shall have praise and many thanks from the management because I have brought to the Château this Louise Martel with the beautiful voice."

Louise flushed with pleasure at hearing her own secret hopes put into words. Since this good chance, as she called it, had come to her, she grew more bright and lighthearted every day. She laughed often. She played with Jou-Jou until his cheeks were as rosy as apples and his eyes shone like stars.

80

The two little rooms in the Street Under-the-Fort were often merry now. It was a far more cheerful and happy spot than it had been in many a long day.

One evening, Louise put on her French peasant dress so that Père Coté and Mère Clotilde might see it before the great night at the Château.

"Is she not beautiful?" cried Madelon, gazing at Louise with admiring eyes. "Never have I seen anyone so beautiful as Louise."

Madelon was right. Louise did look beautiful in the striped skirt, the soft white blouse and black velvet bodice, a white cap with stiff wings on her pretty, fair hair.

"What folly!" said Louise, laughing and shaking her head at Madelon.

But Mère Clotilde did not laugh. She nodded as she turned Louise slowly round and round.

"It is well, both the costume and the girl who wears it," said Mère Clotilde. "But I shall wash and iron the cap and blouse for you myself. The blouse should be very soft, the cap very stiff. I know."

At last, it was the morning of the great day that Louise was to sing at the Château. The sky was heavy and gray. There was a chilly dampness in the air. It was going to snow.

"Do not stumble and fall." Mère Clotilde stood in her doorway with upraised hand. "Do not crush your bundle. There must not be one wrinkle in the cap. Tell Louise that I say so, Madelon."

Madelon nodded. She did not mean to stumble and fall. She would not crush the bundle. She would carry the freshly washed and ironed blouse and cap to Louise with as much care as Mère Clotilde herself.

And so she did. She reached the door of Louise's home without mishap of any kind. Jou-Jou was not in the window.

Harlequin, standing alone, looked out into the street with a pensive air.

In answer to Madelon's knock, Louise opened the door. But it was a different Louise, pale and anxious, with eyelids that were reddened as if she had cried. What had happened to make her look so sad, so worried and full of care?

"Jou-Jou is ill," Louise told Madelon at once. "All night he has suffered with pain in his back and leg. He tosses and is never still. He holds my hand and wishes me to pet and love him every moment. He is not content unless I am with him, close at his side."

All that Louise had said was true. At Jou-Jou's bedside Madelon looked with pity at the little flushed face, at the tiny body that tossed and turned in pain. And always the frail hand clutched Louise, and the little voice called out, "Louise, do not leave me! Stay with me, Louise!"

"Shall I run for Mère Clotilde?" whispered Madelon.

And scarcely waiting for Louise's nod, she was off.

Mère Clotilde looked sober when she reached Jou-Jou's bedside. He did not open his eyes and look at her, though she stiffly sank upon her knees beside him and called him many fond names.

"The doctor, we must have the doctor," said Mère Clotilde at last.

But Louise shook her head.

"I have no money," said Louise, pressing her lips tight. "I cannot pay."

"Chut!" said Mère Clotilde almost angrily. "Why do you talk so when you have friends! I shall send for the doctor and for Père Coté as well."

The doctor came, a pleasant young man who patted Louise's shoulder and playfully shook Jou-Jou's string of buttons in the hope of making him smile.

"I cannot tell the malady for one or two days," he said at last. "It may come from lameness, but I am not sure. Give this medicine, and keep him quiet and warm."

Then Louise asked the question that was in her thoughts and in the mind of Mère Clotilde and Madelon as well, but which no one had put into words.

"Will excitement hurt him? You see how he clings to me. Could I leave him for two hours or three tonight?"

"Louise, come to me," called Jou-Jou's voice. "Do not leave me tonight. You may sing at the Château tomorrow. Do not leave me tonight!"

"It would be far better not to leave him," was the doctor's reply. "Excitement is bad for him. He is very frail. Tomorrow I will see him again."

Louise, on the floor, hid her face in the bedclothes while she stroked and patted Jou-Jou's hand.

It was so that Père Coté found her when he came hurrying in. He had stopped around the corner and brought the white furry dog with the red tongue that Jou-Jou had wished for the New Year.

But the little boy opened his eyes only to smile faintly at Père Coté and close them again.

"Louise will not leave me," he said, reaching for her hand. "She will sing tomorrow at the Château."

"Do not think that now," urged Mère Clotilde. "There is always hope."

"No, not if I have no one to take my place." Louise shook her head. "They will never ask me again. My chance is gone. But I am thinking of Père Coté. They will not be pleased at the Château if he disappoints them. Trouble may come of it. Am I not right, Père Coté?"

Père Coté stood biting his lips. His kind face was full of trouble. In all the years he had served the Château, never had he failed them, never disappointed them until now. Tonight, his great night, when he was to play his fiddle for the lovely Louise Martel to sing—to fail them now! How could he go back to the Château and tell them there would be no entertainment tonight?

"You do not think you could leave?" he asked hesitantly. "Not for two or three hours, if Mère Clotilde took your place?"

"How can I?" was Louise's answer. "How can I leave Jou-Jou when he is sick and in pain? How can I sing and give pleasure when I am so full of care?"

Père Coté had no answers to this. There was no help for it. He must fail the Château!

A little hand pulled at his sleeve, and he looked down at Madelon.

"Do you think anyone would like to see me dance?" asked Madelon timidly. "I should like to help, if I can. Do you not think I might dance tonight at the Château? Might I not tonight in place of Louise?"

Louise lifted her head quickly, Mère Clotilde took a step forward, and Père Coté uttered a great sigh of relief.

He stooped and lifted Madelon in his arms.

"It was the good God or one of his angels who put that thought into your head," said Père Coté solemnly. "Madelon has saved us all!"

Chapter 12

Madelon Dances

IT WAS SNOWING. The air was filled with soft white flakes
that flew about like feathers that left a silvery covering
wherever they came to rest.

The great courtyard at the Château glittered. The snow
powdered the arches. It draped the little balconies and wove
soft hoods for the dormer windows and the pointed roofs.
Lights were blazing in every window, and huge iron lanterns
glowed along the wall. Sleighs, one after another, swept up to
the wide entrance with merry jingling of their bells and in a
moment or two dashed off again.

Père Coté and Madelon came walking through the snow
into the courtyard. He carried his fiddle. She held a small
white parcel in her mittened hand. Up the broad entrance
steps he led her and in at the wide front door.

Within the Château, Madelon looked eagerly about
her. Brilliant lights and soft color, beautiful ladies and fine

gentlemen strolling to and fro, lads dressed in plum color with waistcoats of white, who scurried here and there on errands, all this and more she saw as she walked along holding fast to Père Coté's hand. Madelon felt excited and happy and bright. Her cheeks burned, and she held her head high.

Now Père Coté led her to the room where she was to dance—a large room, with a shining floor and little tables and chairs grouped at one end.

"There, at these tables, the ladies and gentlemen will sit and refresh themselves while you dance," explained Père Coté. "See the stage, Madelon, where you will stand."

At the other end of the room, away from the tables, was a platform draped with soft curtains of velvet.

"You must dance here in the center of the stage," instructed Père Coté, "and I will stand at this side and play for you. Now we will go into this little room off the stage, and I will arrange your costume and put on your cap."

Madelon's costume? Madelon's cap? Surely she had neither when she came to Québec.

That is true. It was only that afternoon that Mère Clotilde had gone to a large box in which she kept many treasures and had taken from it a little French peasant dress that had belonged to her Mimi when she was a little girl.

Madelon had eagerly slipped into the little peasant dress—blue skirt, white blouse, black velvet bodice, and pretty white cap. The dress was a trifle too large, but what was that to Mère Clotilde's skillful fingers? A tuck here, a stitch there, and Mère Clotilde put down her needle with a nod.

"It is well," she said. "Now let me wash and iron the cap and blouse, and Madelon will have a costume worthy of her and Père Coté."

So tonight Madelon wore the costume, and from the white paper parcel, carried so carefully, Père Coté took the stiffly starched little white cap and fitted it upon her dark, curly head.

By that time the musicians for the dance had come into the big room and had seated themselves comfortably below the stage. They tuned their instruments and began to play a lively air.

Now the dancers drifted into the room, and soon could be heard the faint sound of their dancing feet. Madelon could hear laughter and low voices, too, but she could see nothing. Père Coté would not allow her even to peep from behind the velvet curtains.

"You must come as a surprise," said Père Coté firmly.

The music played on and on. Then suddenly it ended with a crash!

Père Coté rose and took his fiddle. Madelon slipped from her seat.

The moment had come for Madelon to dance!

Père Coté, brave in his velveteen jacket, walked out upon the stage, and Madelon followed him.

Oh, how bright and glowing the room looked now! Lights were blazing everywhere. The room was crowded with lovely ladies and fine gentlemen, sitting around the little tables, all laughing and talking in the pleasantest way. The ladies were beautiful, dressed in pale pink and silver and flame color and purest white.

All this Madelon saw as she stood in the center of the stage, a smiling little *habitant* girl, her dark curls showing beneath her stiff, snowy cap, holding out her blue skirt with both her hands, while she waited for Père Coté to draw his bow across the strings.

A nod from Père Coté and in the room, grown quiet, Madelon began to dance.

Lightly, lightly, in answer to the fiddle, Madelon danced to and fro. The fiddle sang up, the fiddle sang down, now fast, now slow, and Madelon tripped brightly in time to its song. Now she fluttered like a leaf blown by the gale, almost coming to rest on the ground, and then twirling off again when a fresh gust came. Now at the sad cry of the birds on her dark northern river, she floated about with outstretched wings, only, at the fiddle's call, to turn into a merry little butterfly, who danced in and out among the flowers faster, faster, faster, until at last the dance ended in a great wide whirl.

The ladies and gentlemen were clapping; they were clapping very loud and very hard. Some of the ladies and gentlemen were standing up. They were coming toward the stage.

At last the dance ended in a great wide whirl.

Madelon looked at Père Coté. He nodded to her that all was well.

So Madelon, flushed and smiling, stood waiting. And when the ladies and gentlemen reached the stage, she stepped forward and took the outstretched hands of a very pretty lady, a lady in palest pink with pale pink cheeks and golden hair and a sweet, sweet smile.

"What a beautiful dance!" said the pretty lady. "Who taught you to dance like that?"

"No one taught me. I know," answered Madelon, "but Père Coté's fiddle sometimes tells me what to do."

"Is Père Coté your father?" asked a gentleman.

And at this Madelon laughed and shook her head.

"No, no, Père Coté is my friend," she said. "My papa is a guide in the woods and a fur trapper too. He has been away trapping for a long, long time, but he will come soon now. I look for him every day."

There were more people now, standing around the stage. They were all smiling at Madelon and looking at her in the most friendly way. They enjoyed her dancing. There was no doubt about that.

"Does the little girl often dance in public?" asked a gentleman of Père Coté.

"Indeed, no, never before," was Père Coté's answer. "There is a reason why she is here tonight."

"I will tell the reason to you," said Madelon. "It is because of Louise and of Jou-Jou, who is very ill. Louise was to sing to you tonight. It was her good chance, and she was very happy, for she is poor. But Jou-Jou, her little brother, fell ill. He is lame; he cannot walk. He is ill, so ill. She could not leave him. How could she? I leave it to you."

"She could not. Indeed, no," agreed the pretty lady in pink. "And so you came to dance in her place?"

"Yes," answered Madelon. "She is my friend."

The pretty lady turned and spoke softly to a friend. He turned to another friend, who nodded and then moved quietly around the room, speaking here and there as he went.

"Is the little girl to dance again?" asked the pretty lady of Père Coté.

"Once more," was his answer. "Then she must go home and to bed."

"May she not dance now, if she is rested?" asked the lady. "We should all like to see her dance again and soon."

So back from the stage a little way stepped the ladies and gentlemen. And Madelon, shaking out her blue skirt, made ready to dance.

Père Coté raised his bow when Madelon, on tiptoe, suddenly cried out:

"Papa! Papa!" cried Madelon, looking toward the door. "My papa has come! Papa, quick, quick!"

With both hands, she threw excited kisses toward Papa, who at last had arrived, who at last had reached Québec from the Great North Woods. And when Mère Clotilde had told him where Madelon was to be found, how she was to dance alone at the great Château, Papa had hurried off in the hope that he might have a glimpse of his little girl. Now he stood in the doorway, smiling, his face growing very red at Madelon's cry while the friendly waiter who had led him there, slipped hastily out of sight.

Papa waved his hand to Madelon and motioned for her to go on with the dance.

But Madelon shook her head.

"Come, Papa, come," she called. "Come, clap and tap for me."

Everyone had turned and was looking at Papa. They all laughed and nodded kindly. They beckoned for him to do as Madelon wished.

So Papa, growing still more red, was forced to walk forward, and at the stage, Madelon threw both arms about his neck and kissed him on either cheek.

"Now, a chair for Papa," said Madelon.

And a chair being brought by one of the laughing gentlemen, Papa, though dressed in his thick sweater and high boots, sat down upon the stage.

Again Madelon took her place. Again Père Coté, his gray hair standing out like a halo, raised his bow, and to the sound of the fiddle and the steady clapping and tapping, Madelon danced her merriest and her best. It was such a bright little jig, with such twinkling of feet and such bobbing of curls, that when Madelon ended, rosy and out of breath, everyone was smiling and nodding and tapping too.

How they clapped for Madelon! Again and again and again! It really seemed as if they would never stop.

When at last they were quiet, the pretty lady took a handkerchief from her friend—a handkerchief which held something heavy and which the lady now tied securely around the top with her own tiny handkerchief, like a cobweb, Madelon thought.

The pretty lady put the handkerchief into Madelon's hands.

"It is a present for your Louise and her little Jou-Jou," said the lady gently. "It is a little present of money that we have given because your dancing pleases us and because you are her friend."

Madelon looked up at the pretty lady.

"I thank you," said Madelon gravely. "Louise will be happy."

Then Madelon turned first to Papa and then to Père Coté to see what she should do next.

"Sing a little song, Madelon, in farewell to the kind ladies and gentlemen," suggested Père Coté. "I will play it for you."

Père Coté's fiddle began the song of Columbine that Madelon had sung so often by the roadside in Tadoussac.

And Madelon sang:

"In the pale moonlight
To thy door I run.
Lend a pen, I pray thee,
Till my task is done.
Candlelight I have none,
Burns my fire no more,
For the love of heaven,
Open now thy door."

The ladies and gentlemen were delighted with the song. They clapped their hands, they fluttered their handkerchiefs like so many little birds, and they clapped again.

Madelon made a bow. She threw kisses with both her hands. She was very happy.

But now she stood alone upon the stage. It was time to go. One last kiss that flew straight to the pretty lady in pink, and amid the clapping of hands and fluttering of handkerchiefs, Madelon ran off the stage into Papa's arms.

Her dance at the Château was over!

Spring had come, and Captain Le Bel's little boat made its way down the St. Lawrence River and into the harbor at Tadoussac.

On the wharf stood Madame Pinaud, and beside her, in a row, were Oncle Paul and Tante Marie, holding baby Victorine, and Hector and André and Germaine and little Bernadette. They were all looking at the deck of the boat, and, as it came nearer, four people could be plainly seen, leaning against the rail.

There was Madelon, wrapped in the scarlet cape, holding fast to Papa's hand, and on the other side of Papa stood

Louise—yes, Louise—though she was so rosy and smiling it was hard to believe one's eyes. Beside Louise stood a little form who, even as they looked, walked slowly round and took his place at Madelon's side. Who could that be? Not Jou-Jou surely, for he could not walk.

As the boat drew into the wharf, Madelon, smiling and waving, called out to her friends.

"My papa! Do you see my papa?" called Madelon. "And my new maman, Louise. Yes, Louise! She is now my maman. She is coming home with us now to St. Alphonse to live."

Madelon paused to laugh happily, but only for a moment.

"And Jou-Jou, the little Jou-Jou," she called again, "do you see that he walks? Walk, Jou-Jou, walk!"

Up the deck went Jou-Jou, walking bravely, his little leg in an iron brace.

"You see, he walks," went on Madelon triumphantly. "He will grow stronger and better every day. The great doctor has said it. It is the great doctor in Québec whom my papa took to little Jou-Jou. It is well. Is it not true?"

And having told all the news in a breath, Madelon ran to help Jou-Jou back to the rail while her elders talked for the few moments that the boat was to stay in Tadoussac if it hoped to reach St. Alphonse before night fell.

Now, with wavings and farewells, the boat slid out of the harbor and turned on its journey up the dark Saguenay River.

And as long as the boat was in sight, Madelon, bright Madelon, could be seen at the rail, her scarlet cape fluttering in the wind, throwing kisses to her friends with both her hands.

The End